Alain Badan · Spiritual Identity

AF143621

FSC
www.fsc.org

MIXTE

Papier issu
de sources
responsables
Paper from
responsible sources

FSC® C105338

Alain Badan

Spiritual
identity

beyond our identities

Silence Is Eternal Eloquence

Beyond words, the Ultimate Reality.

© 2014, Alain Badan
Published by Books on Demand,
12/14 rond-point des Champs-Elysées,
75008 Paris, France
Printed by Books on Demand GmbH,
Norderstedt, Germany
Legal deposit: January 2014
ISBN: 9782322027767

Preface

Dear reader,

In this book, I invite you on a journey out of the ordinary. An adventure which goes much further than words. Much further than our intellectual, logical understanding.

This journey will lead you to share with me in an adventure which took me well beyond the limits of human experience, to what is deepest in each one of us and only yearns to blossom, to bloom, like the lotus expressing all its beauty on the silt of human passions. Beyond the physical, human journey that I made and that I tell in my own words, this adventure led me to the Spiritual Experience, the Experience of the Ultimate Reality of the Universe and of ourselves, the Experience of One's Divine Self.

The words in this book are only the means by which I have tried to transmit, as faithfully and sincerely as possible, the experience of a reality which IS, a reality well beyond words, well beyond logic.

A journey which led me to a Life, a Love, a Happiness, a Peace and a Freedom which exceed human understanding.

To understand this book, you should not try to understand the words as in a novel, for instance, but rather allow yourself to be carried along by the words. Let yourself go on a journey, a physical, human and spiritual adventure which will lead you further than hope, well beyond what we can understand, conceive, imagine and dream with our five senses, in the state of human consciousness,; a journey which surpasses our ordinary logic and brings us to another understanding of Life, the Universe and ourselves.

So there we go, I wish you a very pleasant journey.

The Stages Of The Journey:

Introduction

*G*od, Salvation, Heaven, the Promised Land, Celestial Jerusalem, Nirvana, the Sacred Land of Islam, Tao, Self-awareness, Cosmic Consciousness, Christ like Consciousness, Divine Consciousness, the Void, the Awakening, the Illumination, the Absolute, the Ultimate Reality, that Without a Name, that Without Shape, the Non-Dual, That, the Divine Self.

Have these apparently different expressions something in common?

In terms of the words, they seem very different and each one seems to have its own meaning. But are words the Truth?

For a very long time, people have been tearing one another apart about the Truth, because they are bound up in the letter of the spirit, rather than understanding the spirit of the letter. They take words, books, speeches and beliefs for Truth.

Because they have not experienced the Divine. They have only read books or listened to speeches and believe that they know the Truth. But Truth can only be known by experiencing the Impersonal personally, just as we cannot know what a piece of fruit tastes like by listening to someone speak about it, or by reading a description of it. Only by tasting the fruit can we really know what the fruit tastes like.

Philosophy, science, religion, spirituality.

Philosophers make beautiful speeches and construct doctrines, but they go no further than words. They do not know the real taste of the Divine fruit.

Religions teach us to believe in a God that we cannot know in this world, but that we will perhaps know in the hereafter. Their original message has been lost in the mist of time and of the human spirit. They have become mere belief systems, liable to conflict with one another.

Science tries to understand the Truth in an intellectual, logical fashion. It tries to understand the outside appearance of the universe and life with sophisticated instruments, using logic and mathematics.

Spirituality teaches the Truth through experience of the Divine, the Ultimate Reality, our Universal and Eternal Identity beyond our human, religious, cultural, racial, national and social identities.

Through this account of an experience of the Ultimate Reality, I invite you to share this experience and undertake, with me, this journey towards the Universal and Absolute Source of Creation and of ourselves.

Each one of us will be led through this experience one day, in this life or in another.

It is our ultimate destiny, the return to the Supreme Source, to Heaven. To Love, to Happiness, to Peace and to Perfect, Eternal and Indestructible Freedom. We are all, already here and now, in the depths of our being.

However, we forgot this a long time ago. All that is left is this deep, unfocused nostalgia of a blessed time, a heavenly state.

Before the experience

1985 was the year when I discovered Japan, a country where modernity is still impregnated with ancestral traditions and a deep, rich spiritual culture; a country where the ancient and modern live in perfect harmony.

I arrived in Japan in May 1985, with 200 dollars in my pocket and a heavy dose of optimism, and with a friend I had met in Bangkok a few weeks beforehand. He had already worked in Japan in 1984 and assured me that it was easy to find work there.

Having arrived in Tokyo, he went to work in the hotel that had taken him on the year before. He offered to look after my travel bag while I found a room and a job. His place of work was in Roppongi, a trendy district in the Japanese capital.

There I was with 200 dollars in my pocket, in the middle of a country I knew nothing about, in a megalopolis of 12 million inhabitants at the time, with the main aim of finding a room and a job as quickly as possible. This would help me get by and allow me to continue my journey.

I spent my days talking to many expatriates in Roppongi, the district where most gaijins (people from outside of Japan) were, ever in the hope of finding a room and a job as soon as possible, a search which had become almost an obsession.

My days were always interesting, full of pleasant encounters with people whose lives were rich in adventures and experiences. Like me, many of them were travellers looking for something different, another way of life, another direction from what was available in human society.

I slept wherever I could – the entrance halls of buildings, staircases, stations, sometimes amid a bit of greenery in a park.

Several times a week, I met the friend I had come with to this other world, which Japan was for me at that time. He would ask how I was getting on and I used to go for a shower where he worked.

The days were passing, my meagre financial resources were dwindling away and there was still no room or job in sight.

A fortnight later, I was thin, tired and becoming more and more desperate. My friend told me that one of his friends, an expatriate, had a room to let and that he knew the Japanese manager of a German brasserie who was looking for a barman.

At last, I was able to see a brighter future. The room was basic but comfortable, in a little wooden, two-floored house, with a toilet in the corridor, near the entrance. No shower. I had to go to the Sento (Japanese public baths) every day, just under a kilometre away. The district was called Omotesando, near Shibuya. In those days, it was a quiet place with small, traditional houses, tiny Japanese restaurants and a few little bars and shops.

After I had dropped my things off and had a wash, I went to introduce myself at the German brasserie, which was situated near the American embassy in the district of Akasaka, a long way from where I was living.

The boss, a very pleasant, pretty woman of about forty, introduced me to the staff and filled me in on the details of my work and the pay: 1000 yen an hour, or about 10 Swiss francs at that time. No CV, no contract, just a hand-shake.

The restaurant opened from 6pm to midnight during the week and until 2am on Fridays and Saturdays.

Tokyo people generally work very hard during the week, rest or have parties on Friday evenings and Saturdays and sleep on Sundays. Hence the restaurant was closed on Sundays, meaning I could use this to recover from six days' intense work.

Later on, I also had the chance to play many bit-parts in Japanese films, even in an adaptation of the film 'Cabaret', with a Japanese Liza Minnelli. I also made an advertisement for a Japanese television channel, with a rock group in which I played the role of a bassist. This was a very amusing experience, as I had never held a guitar before in my life. A dentist also asked me to give her French lessons once a week.

6 months passed between work, discovering the Japanese people and Japan itself, beautiful encounters and a stressful life. It was a difficult experience, but very enriching on a personal level.

By the beginning of November 1985, I had saved enough money to continue my journey through Asia and on to Australia, so I took a plane for Bangkok, in Thailand.

After six months' hard work, I decided to spend some time on an island in the south of Thailand, in order to relax and think about the next stage of the journey.

After a few weeks spent resting on the beach and eating well, I decided to begin my leisurely journey down to Australia by road, train and boat.

I took the train from Surat Thani, in the south of Thailand, for Penang, an island in the north-west of Malaysia, near the border with Thailand. From there, a boat took me to Medan, in the north-east of Sumatra in Indonesia. After a few days spent visiting the place,

I took a minibus to Padang, a little further to the south on the west coast.

The driver was a middle-aged Muslim and, like me, was not particularly talkative, but it was a long journey and we ended up chatting a little about our respective lives and the Indonesian people. During the trip, we arrived at a wayside mosque. He asked me politely if he could stop to pray. I was touched by his request and waited patiently in the minibus, contemplating the scene around me. After a few more pleasant hours on the road, we finally reached Padang, on the west coast of Sumatra. I spent a few days wandering around the picturesque streets and trying the excellent, spicy cuisine.

I then left Padang by minibus, stopping here and there along the road to admire the beauty of the southern part of Sumatra.

After several days on the road, broken up by short stays in small local guest houses, called losmens, I finally arrived in Jakarta, the capital of Indonesia, where I stayed a few days.

One evening, while I was walking in a back street near the losmen where I was staying, I came across two young Indonesians who, after saying hello, asked me to buy them a beer. As they did not seem particularly threatening, I went along with it. It was a beautiful evening of sharing and friendship at a quiet café, with a few pleasant bystanders who came over now and again to share a laugh or a few words.

After Jakarta, I carried on to Bogor, a lovely, quiet little town with a pretty nature reserve, and then on to Bandung, a small provincial town on the island of Java, to the south of Jakarta.

Bandung, letting go completely

*I*n those days, Bandung was a quiet little town with a river running through it, without any particular charm.

In one place, a little arched bridge allows pedestrians to cross to the other side. To this day, this bridge remains a symbol for me of the passage to the other side of ourselves, towards our Infinite, Immortal Being, and the beginning of a spiritual adventure that led me to the experience of Ultimate Reality.

One morning, I set foot on this bridge for the first time. When I reached the middle of the bridge, at its highest point, an energy of power, peace, softness, tenderness and infinite love completely enfolded me and penetrated to the deepest point of my being. This energy was at once around me and in me. My body stopped walking in the middle of the bridge and this sublime energy asked me, without a word but in a kind of soul to soul dialogue, with perfect unity although there was no duality between us, to let go of everything – my physical body, my desires, my own life and the very idea of my journey.

I remember saying, inside myself: "OK, I've got my passport and some traveller's cheques to get home to Switzerland, if need be." And at that moment, I gave myself over completely, totally and in absolute trust to this sublime energy. From that moment on, it guided my steps and I was freed from all cares and worries. A deep peace overcame me. The past and the future no longer had any importance; I was living in the Eternal Present, Here and Now.

I had become like a new-born child, fully appreciating each moment of this life which was given to me. I quietly went on my way, by minibus and train, through the beauty of the landscapes and villages of that region of Java.

Then I arrived at Yogyakarta, half way along the west coast of the island. This little provincial town, picturesque and full of charm, is a centre for the creation of batik, a technique of printing on fabrics. The inhabitants of the region, like all the Indonesians I met, are extremely kind, gentle and welcoming. I stayed several days among them, sharing some beautiful moments. I hired rickshaws to take in batik workshops and the peaceful charm of the place, with its lively little streets and picturesque houses. Sometimes, I ventured out of town to admire the sublime beauty of the verdant paddy fields, which seemed to cover the country with a beautiful blanket of harmony.

One day, I rented a motorbike to go down to the seaside, to a place called Parangtritis. It must have developed since then, but at that time it was a little fishing village by a dangerous sea, where rolling waves crashed loudly onto the shore. If you went too far from the beach, powerful currents swept you out to sea, with no hope of returning. I briefly experienced it one day when I swam too far out. I suddenly felt that I was being carried out to sea. Swimming as forcefully as I could, I finally made it to the shore. Evidently, my time for leaving this world had not yet come.

I spent a few more days riding around the surrounding area by motorbike. The place is really stunning, its luxuriant nature dotted with pretty little villages and beautiful verdant paddy fields.

After several happy, peaceful days in Yogyakarta, I caught a plane for Bali, or "the island of the gods", as it is called by its inhabitants. When I arrived at Denpasar airport, I took a taxi to the tourist beach at Legian, near Kuta. I found a little losmen, an Indonesian guest house, a stone's throw away from the sea.

The place was nice and the Balinese people were gentle, welcoming and pleasant. I divided a few peaceful days between the beach, walks and sharing good times with the Balinese.

I then left by minibus for Candi Dasa, further north on the east coast. At that time, it was a little fishing village by a turquoise sea, where a few restaurants and losmens welcomed hippies or travellers on a low budget, like me.

I found a lovely private chalet with a little patio, just by the sea. The place was peaceful and beautiful and I decided to spend a few days there.

Each morning, even before my alarm went off, breakfast was served on a tray, left on the table on the little patio. There was a flask of tea or coffee, toast and fruit – one of the beautiful Indonesian customs.

The Spiritual Experience

One morning, I decided to rent a little motorbike to have a look round the island. The person renting the bikes gave me the only one he had left, a good old Japanese model which must have been twenty years old and been up and down all the roads on the island many, many times. After checking that everything was in working order, I paid what I owed, climbed onto the bike and set off along the coast road towards the north of the island.

The weather was glorious, with an ideal temperature and breathtakingly beautiful landscapes. So as to admire, or rather contemplate, the sublime beauty around me, I decided to ride as slowly as possible, about 10 or 15 km/hour, according to the venerable speedometer which, curiously, still worked.

The road was narrow and poorly maintained; I sometimes had to avoid potholes or vehicles coming the other way.

From the start of this ride round the island, I was in a meditative frame of mind. It was not a mere ride, but a meditation. I was in a state of deep peace, without cares, without worries of any sort. My spirit was totally calm. I was living for the present moment, here and now.

I rode through wonderful landscapes. On my left, I saw magnificent mountains, covered with terraces of sublime paddy fields and, on my right, vines on stakes by a turquoise sea. This magnificent landscape was not something separate from me, I was part of it. I was in perfect harmony with everything surrounding me.

During my peaceful, meditative ride, I stopped for a

moment here and there at the roadside, without getting off the motorbike, so as to enter into deeper communion with everything around me.

Then I came to a place where men were hard at work repairing the road. I slowed down to see what they were doing. They looked at me briefly, waved me through and returned to their heavy work.

The sun was now at its peak. A gentle warmth enveloped me and the sublime beauty of the place seeped ever further into my whole being.

The journey was more and more beautiful and more and more intense. Life flowed through every cell in my body and through my whole being.

At one point, something on my right caught my eye, a place that seemed a little strange. It was a sort of small valley which rolled softly 150 or 200 metres down to the sea. Right at the bottom was a lonely house by a little beach. I don't know why, but I felt that I had to stop there a long while. I was intrigued by the lonely house. I stayed looking at it a long time. A little path led down through the small valley as far as the house. Part of me wanted to go down and visit whoever lived there. But I could not make up my mind to go down. I could not take my eyes off the house. The idea came to me that maybe a Wise Man lived there. I stood there for a long time, so it seemed, without being able to make my mind up.

Then, little by little, the attraction for the place slowly lifted and I continued my meditative ride. I would never know who the house was inhabited by, if even at all, but the moment and the image of that place have remained forever fixed in my mind.

The road rolled out in front of me, through ever more magnificent landscapes. I was still chugging along on my old machine at 10 – 15 km/hour when, seemingly for a fraction of a second, everything around me went completely black. The world as I had seen it up to then had totally disappeared. Then, suddenly, I emerged into a Sublime White Light, a new state of consciousness, a new state of being where everything was Perfect Light, Perfect Unity, Perfect Life. Human forms, nature, trees, plants, animals and stones were, in truth, Light. Their shapes were still there but were no longer living by themselves. They were a manifestation of Life and of the Eternal and Universal Light that animates all things.

Everything was now bathed in Perfect Light, Life, Harmony and Unity. And I gradually became aware of the fact that I, too, as a physical body, a human being, was a manifestation and expression of this Life and Infinite Light.

But I was also infinitely more than this mortal body, this little human personality. I was Soul or Divine fragment. I was also this Light, this infinite Life. I was the life of all Lives. I was the other human being, nature, the animal, the tree, the flower, the blade of grass, the grain of sand, the stone, the mountain, the ocean, the stars in the universe, the whole universe and much more besides. I was Infinite, Unlimited.

There were no more thoughts, no more breathing, no more emotions. I was beyond the mind, beyond breathing, beyond emotions, beyond the duality of good and evil, man and woman, darkness and light, beyond life and death. In One's Supreme Self, the Ultimate Reality. In the Absolute Evidence.

I was bathed in a Silence of Unfathomable Depth and Intensity, which is Eternal Eloquence. That Silence taught me without words, by deliciously intense waves of Love and Bliss. It Is Infinite Presence. Perfect Peace. In a Perfect Unity, it made me aware that I am Soul,

Infinite, Unlimited, Immortal, Eternal, Indestructible. Eternally and perfectly happy, peaceful and free.

All cares, all thoughts, all worries, all fears and all desires had completely disappeared. The very idea of death no longer existed. The past and future were no more. I also became aware that in this blessed state, I was beyond space and time. I was at once point A and point B and beyond. I was omnipresent. I was eternal.

I was in the eternal present, Here and Now.

I understood that what is called life and what is called death, in the state of human consciousness, are the two facets of the same Eternal and Universal Life in this relative dimension of existence. Of space-time.

I was perfectly detached from everything, absolutely everything. Not only things which seem so important in this life and in this world, but also from what is called life and what is called death in the state of human consciousness.

I was also aware that down, way down, far from the Immensity of the Being that I AM, (that we all are, in truth), a tiny dark spot, which had been my me, and which was now no more than a pile of matter, was moving slowly along on a tiny motorbike. That tiny body had been me, but was no longer me, it was the Evidence itself, the Absolute Evidence. I was perfectly free of it. If it had been burnt, crushed, cut into pieces or given to animals to eat, I would have felt no pain, no frustration, no discomfort and no anxiety. None of that was important any more. It was quite simply no longer me.

Nowadays, I realise that this body is just a vehicle allowing the Divine Soul, that we all are, to be incarnate in this world, in this space-time, for a short period of time. A garment we put on at birth and which we cast off when it is worn out, in a process we call death.

What I really am, what we all really are, is Evidence

itself. The rest, this body, this human life in space-time, is an illusion stemming from our attachment to the body and from our ignorance of our true spiritual nature.

All desires had totally disappeared. Love, Happiness, Peace and the perfect, eternal and indestructible Freedom in which I was submerged had no beginning and no end and could not be destroyed, as they are the very nature of Life, one's Divine Self.

I was perfectly satisfied and would have liked to live in that state for all eternity, whatever the physical and human condition. Nothing else mattered any more. I did not have love, happiness, peace and freedom to be taken away or destroyed. I was Love, Happiness, Peace and perfect, eternal and indestructible Freedom.

When we are in this state of Perfect Bliss, in the Ultimate Reality of the universe and ourselves, at the Ultimate Spiritual Source of all life and all creation, what we call reality in the state of human consciousness, in our ignorance, is a dream. And the ultimate aim of us all, in this life or in another, is to awaken from this dream and to reach what is, for the one who has awoken, one's true nature, the Absolute Evidence, the Ultimate Reality.

But there is nothing to reach which has not already been there for all eternity. Nothing to create which has not been created for all eternity.

I do not know how this body arrived in Singaraja, a little town in the north of Bali. Even after years of thought and reflection, I am convinced that Universal Life and the Absolute took total control of my body and guided me there. I can find no other explanations.

I stopped at a little supermarket to buy a drink. At the exit, I happened upon a child who looked about fifteen and whose face was completely deformed. His face was something like an elephant's. I was deeply touched to see that he lived in great unhappiness, due of course to his illness, but also to the fact that he was convinced, in his ignorance and attachment, that his body, that deformed face before me, was his me, his true identity. I wanted to go up to him and say, "look, you are not this deformed body, you too are Immortal Soul, you too are already, here and now, Love, Happiness, Peace and Perfect Freedom."

But the Universal Life which had guided me there turned my attention away from that unfortunate boy and I went on my way. He went towards his destiny. He had to live through his experiences. One day, he too will experience Perfect Love, Perfect Happiness, Perfect Peace and Ultimate Freedom. He too will know his true Identity. He too will one day experience Ultimate Reality. He too will know his true Self.

This is the ultimate aim of all of us, whoever we are or believe we are in this life.

Back on my old motorbike, I left Singaraja to return to the south of the island, along one of the two roads that cross Bali from north to south through the mountains. I moved progressively inland, along a little winding road that climbed gently up the mountains. I rode through magnificent landscapes dotted with terraces of paddy fields, forests and mountain valleys sheltering little villages, seemingly resting in peace in those beautiful surroundings. Everything was bathed in serene beauty.

As I rode quietly along, I became aware that I was beyond the cycle of reincarnations, the cycle of successive births and deaths. It is impossible to describe with words. Quite simply, I saw and knew it in the deepest part of my being.

At one point, I decided to stop and admire the way I had come. The view of the road, winding down towards the bottom of the valley, towards the infinite ocean, plunged me into profound contemplation. I do not know how long I stayed there.

As if from nowhere, a young man suddenly appeared on my left. Humbly and silently, he looked at me and held out his hand to ask for a coin. I took a coin out of my pocket and gave it to him. He nodded his thanks and went on his way. Still today, I do not know where he came from. There was no path on my left, no house as far as the eye could see and, a few moments after turning away, he had completely disappeared from view.

My old motorbike was inexhaustible. It took me up to an isolated pass in the middle of a heavenly mountain landscape. On the other side, I saw a lake, further down in the distance, and decided to go there. After a few kilometres along a small, winding road, I finally came to the lakeside.

The water was calm and clear and the place was permeated with a serene beauty, shaded with a touch of mystery. A few hundred metres away to my left, I noticed an old wooden temple by the lakeside and I decided to go there. It was a little temple, all made of wood in the Balinese style, decorated with magnificent sculptures. The perfectly still water of the lake reflected the beauty of the temple and the surrounding mountains. The atmosphere was permeated with mystery and great serenity.

I edged round the lake along a little path and finally came to a small restaurant with a pretty terrace by the water. They served a Balinese buffet. At the sight of such beautiful colours, my attention was drawn to these earthly foods and their fragrances quickly reminded me that it was time to feed my body.

After tasting some of the dishes and embracing the

calm of the area, I headed off again. After a certain time climbing the winding road I saw, in the distance, a valley descending towards the south.

The sky slowly clouded over and a light rain accompanied me for the last part of the journey. The road was long, downhill all the way, leading through little villages or past isolated houses, seemingly floating on magnificent terraces of paddy fields. People were simply going about their business.

I arrived at last at the bottom of the valley and quickly reached the coast road. Now I only had to ride back to Candi Dasa. Night fell during the last stage of the trip and, after returning the old motorbike, I arrived at my chalet during the night. I was exhausted. I had a shower and fell into a deep sleep.

The following days were given over quite simply to living. I was still permeated by my sublime spiritual experience and spent my days between bathing in a turquoise sea, decorated with magnificent corals and fish of all colours, pleasant times shared with very friendly Balinese people and some delicious cooking.

After several days' intense living, without fears or cares, in happiness, peace and intense freedom, bathed in the unity of all things, I decided to leave for Australia in the hope of earning a bit of money to continue my journey.

Australia

I took a plane for Darwin, in the north of Australia. At that time, it was a little Australian town with a pretty pedestrianised town centre. I spent a few days there looking for work, unsuccessfully.

I therefore decided to continue my journey and took a coach for Townsville, via Mount Isa. This led me across a large part of the north of the country. Around half-way, we stopped at Mount Isa, in the middle of the desert. When I stepped off the air-conditioned coach, I felt as though I were entering a sauna. The heat was almost unbearable. It must have been about 45 degrees, if not more.

Looking around me, I saw that the place rather resembled a ghost town, like in a western. A few houses, a petrol station, a little grocer's and a little restaurant. It all gave a feeling of being lost in the middle of nowhere.

I bought a sandwich and a drink and went out for a look round. I really was right in the middle of a desert. Only the road disappearing into the distance of the infinite landscape seemed to connect us to the world of the living.

I was overcome by the heat and took refuge on the coach. It left a little later, with its consignment of travellers. The road seemed never-ending and, in places, the landscapes we drove through reminded me somewhat of the moonscapes that I had seen on television.

After what felt like an endless journey, we finally arrived in Townsville, on the east coast of Australia.

In those days, Townsville was a pretty provincial township with wooden, Victorian-style houses, small roads bordered by arcades, little shops, hotels and restaurants.

I took a room in a little wooden, two-floored hotel. The first-floor room was basic but comfortable. A balcony ran right round the building and, from it, one could admire the town and the surroundings.

It was a very pretty place with very friendly people. I decided to spend a few days there and to find out if there was any work to be had.

After a few very pleasant days, with no job on the horizon, I took a coach for Mackay, on the road to Brisbane. There was no work in Mackay either, so I took a coach inland, hoping to make a little money on a fruit or cotton plantation.

By early evening, I came to a campsite in the middle of a cotton plantation. I found a little caravan to spend the night in.

I took my toilet bag and went to the nearby shower block. I stood in front of the mirror to shave and looked at my face. In an instant, like lightning, the Evidence of my true Identity burst forth from the depths of my being. But no, I am not this image in the mirror, the image the mirror is reflecting is not me! It is only an illusion, a pile of matter. I am infinitely more.

After a good shower, I fell into a deep sleep.

The next morning, I asked the campsite owner if there was any work available picking cotton. He answered, with a smile, that the harvest had just finished.

I therefore decided to continue my journey towards Brisbane, further south along the coast.

I spent several pleasant days in that beautiful town. I even had the opportunity to visit the universal exhibition. But after several days' searching, there was still no work on the horizon.

Regretfully, then, I left for Sydney. The wish to work

in Australia lessened from day to day and I decided to go home, to Switzerland, where I would have a greater chance of finding work.

Return to Switzerland

*A*fter my journey, lasting over 19 months and taking me to the other side of the world and to the far reaches of the universe and myself, I came home with pleasure, to my family and friends.

However, I was not ready at this point to speak about my spiritual experience. Only today, 27 years later, do I feel mature enough to attest to it and share with you, dear reader, this spiritual experience that we all live through every day, whoever we are or believe ourselves to be today, in this life, or in a future incarnation. It is the ultimate destiny of each one of us. Or, to use the language of religion, the return to heaven. Or, as Buddha said: one day, all beings will reach Nirvana.

I found work in Geneva within a fortnight, painting buildings.

A curious detail: the district of Geneva where I worked is called 'The end of the world' and the house was used for end-of-life care. In other words, for people who were about to be freed from their illusory, temporary, limited and mortal self and from a pile of matter which had become useless.

In the wilderness

27 years have passed since that sacred day at the beginning of 1986, when I had the supreme blessing, the infinite luck of living through the Spiritual Experience.

Back in the state of human consciousness, in this body, everyday life progressively returned to normal, with its frustrations, failures and ordeals in all aspects of human life.

The failures were mounting up, be they sentimental, professional or financial.

My personal life was becoming more and more frustrating. Nothing seemed to work out the way I wanted, whether it be a business website project into which I put all my effort, job hunting, or setting up a business with other people, nothing worked. I did my best, even more than was expected of me, but the result was always the same: failure.

Then came the ordeal, the terrible ordeal. A failure in my love life. I fell madly in love with a woman who, it was clear to me, was the woman of my life.

Faced with the increasing intensity of my love for her and her ever-firmer refusal, the pain grew ever more intense and sharp, until the winter's day when she pronounced the fatal words: "I don't love you." At that moment, the earth gave way beneath my feet. Life, the world, nothing mattered any more. The suffering was so intense that I wobbled on my trembling legs. All I wanted to do was die and leave this life and cruel world forever.

It took a long time, several years, before I recovered from that painful ordeal.

The idea of ending it all crossed my mind several times. But each time, my conscience told me, "No, don't do it, be brave, you'll come out of the tunnel, one day you'll understand."

That very, very long time in the wilderness lasted nearly 19 years.

Then, over the last few years, slowly, progressively, I have begun to understand the profound meaning of all those years of frustration, unhappiness, failures and ordeals.

On a wall of the wise man Sri Ramana Maharishi's ashram, at the foot of the sacred mountain of Arunachala, in the south of India, is written: 'the ego is the source of all evils'.

The Spiritual Experience is an egoless state.

The greatest danger after living through the Spiritual Experience is of the ego taking over and proclaiming itself master. That would open the door to all the forms of abuse, the deviances and all the aberrations that have been seen, and can still be seen nowadays, throughout the history of humanity on every continent.

There are more blind people leading the blind than authentic Masters capable of guiding the disciple towards Spiritual Awakening and Self-Realisation.

I understood more and more clearly that this long series of negatives was, in reality, positive. Its aim was to purify me of all that was preventing the Divine Self from shining in all its Splendour and hindering me in breaking loose from the ego, source of all evils.

Still today, this process of purification, of transcendence of the ego, is continuing.

The aim of spiritual evolution is not to inflate and satisfy the ego, but to transcend it, to go past it, so that the Divine Self may shine.

The Spiritual Experience leads us to discover,

through life experience, the Splendour of an egoless state and our true Identity.

The long period in the wilderness, the ordeals, the failures and the frustrations cleanse us thoroughly. They detach us progressively from the ego and free us from its burden, from the cause of all suffering, from the tiny dark stain in the Infinity of the Divine Self. It detaches us from our illusory me and destroys what is our own creation, thereby uniting us with Divine Creation.

To fill a glass with pure water, you must first empty it completely of all the impure water it contains.

To live permanently in the Spiritual Experience, the ego must give way to the Divine Self once and for all.

We must transcend our illusory, mortal and temporary identity in order to fulfil our True, Immortal and Eternal Identity.

Indeed, throughout those long and painful years, Life was asking me: "Do you want to carry on living in the illusion that you are this little, limited, imperfect and mortal human personality? Do you want to carry on living with imperfect, unsatisfying and limited love, happiness, peace and freedom, or do you want to live with Love, Happiness, Peace and Freedom in the Splendour of the Indestructible, Infinite, Immortal and Eternal Divine Self?"

As far as I am concerned, such is the profound meaning of that long and painful time in the wilderness.

The message

Whoever we are or believe we are in this life, what are we looking for through thousands of different things?

Love, Happiness, Peace and Perfect, Indestructible, Eternal Freedom.

The paradox is that inside, at the deepest point within ourselves, we are already what we are blindly seeking outside.

From birth, we have to look outwards, to develop our ego, our human me in order to survive in society and find our place in this world.

We learn how to understand things with our five senses.

The more we identify with this body and human personality, the more we look outward, the further we move away from our true being of the Divine Self and from our true Spiritual Identity, whose nature is Love, Happiness, Peace and Perfect Freedom. Or, to use the language of religions, the further we move away from Heaven.

The more we identify with this imperfect, illusory personality, the more unsatisfied, unhappy and imprisoned by this mortal self we become.

Ever more unhappy and tormented, we desperately seek scraps of this Love, Happiness, Peace and lost Freedom in multiple things, in the other.

We mistakenly believe that the other will be the source of our love and happiness. That such or such social standing will bring us more love, happiness, peace and freedom.

Admittedly, these scraps of love, happiness, peace and freedom may last a while and satisfy us for a certain time but, like a shooting star, they always end up disappearing and disappointing us, because such is the nature of things in this world, in the state of human consciousness. Nothing lasts, everything changes. We will never be fully satisfied.

In our ignorance of our Spiritual Identity, we become more and more unhappy, unsatisfied, tormented and desperate.

We forget who we really are. We lose the Original Heaven.

Then one day, in this life or in another, we begin to understand that we are at a dead end, that Truth lies elsewhere and we start to search for what we believe we have lost.

We become searchers. We come ever closer to what we really are deep within ourselves.

Life reveals itself to us in different forms. Books, speeches, a master incarnated in a human body or not, events, encounters, experiences, which lead us little by little on a return journey to our real Self, our true Identity beyond our temporary and illusory identities.

Some go down a religious path, others stay outside of any system of belief and others still take a mystical, spiritual direction.

All those paths have one aim, which is to prepare for the eventual Spiritual Experience. The Experience of the Divine Self, our true Identity, the Ultimate Reality of the Universe and of ourselves. The experience of Love, Happiness, Peace and Perfect, Indestructible and Eternal Freedom.

Then we Know and this Knowledge, born of personal experience, can be taken away by no one; nothing and no one can destroy it, for eternity.

We are beyond hope because there is no longer an ego to hope with. Because we are, once again, what we have hoped to be for so long.

There is no longer any path or goal to reach. We are at once the path and the goal. Beyond space and time.

There is no more belief because we are what we believed in and much, much more. There is no longer an ego to believe in something it cannot grasp.

There is no more birth or death. Only Eternity IS in all its Splendour.

There are no more desires, because there is no more ego to desire anything. No more ego to desire Love, Happiness, Peace or Freedom.

And finally, a great paradox, there is no longer a searcher. Admittedly, we must begin by becoming searchers and searching for what we forgot a very long time ago, our true Identity or Divine Self. But one day, when we are ready, the searcher must let go completely and disappear to let the Divine Self shine in all its Splendour.

Then there is no more searcher to search, no more object of the search. No more path to follow. We are beyond the searcher, beyond the search, beyond the path, beyond time and space.

The searcher's complete letting-go could be described with this image: jumping off a high mountain, but instead of dropping into the void, we rise up in trust, towards the Light. We become Everything, the Infinite, the Life of all lives.

Once the Spiritual Experience has erased all trace of attachment, all trace of illusion, of separation, of belief, of need of hope, of desires and of fears, only the Divine Self shines, our true Identity, which is eternally Love, Happiness, Peace and Perfect Freedom.

It is the apocalypse. The end of all illusions and the revelation of the Ultimate Reality, the Divine Self.

It is the return to the Heaven of religions. Whatever name we give to the Unspeakable. Whatever description we can give of the Indescribable.

All traces of impurity have completely disappeared. Only the Divine Self shines again in all its Splendour, eternally.

It is the end of the journey, the end of the cycle of births and deaths.

It is the return to our original state. The return to Heaven.

The Indians have a beautiful formula for expressing this state of being and of perfect detachment: I AM, neither this, nor that.

The apocalypse

*A*pocalypse comes from the Greek word meaning Revelation.

Revelation comes from Spiritual Experience.

Spiritual Experience is not in books or speeches. It is in the personal experience of the Ultimate Reality, the Divine Self, the Truth, our true Identity. In the personal experience of the Impersonal.

The spiritual domain is so subtle that it is very easy to have a mistaken understanding of it and come to the wrong conclusions.

The Source of Creation and of ourselves is beyond the mental, beyond the five senses. Beyond this mortal body. Wanting to 'understand' it with our intellect, our logic, our thought, 'imagine' it with our imagination, is like trying to describe the Indescribable, name the Unnameable, imagine the Unimaginable, limit the Unlimited, shut the Infinite in a little box.

Believing that the apocalypse is the destruction of the world, so that the master of such and such a religion can come back to Earth, is certainly a mistaken understanding of the apocalypse.

The apocalypse is not an event in time – past, present or future. It is a spiritual event which can happen at any moment, here and now, in the life of every human being, whether atheist or believer, whichever system of belief they follow, or not.

The apocalypse is not the destruction of the world but the transcendence of the ego and of illusions. The illusion of believing that this world is reality. The illusion of believing that this body, this human personality, is our real identity, our true Self. The illusion of believing that our system of belief, whichever one it is, is the Truth. The illusion of believing that books and speeches are the truth.

Once we have the supreme blessing and infinite luck of the Spiritual Experience, all illusions and attachment disappear completely and the Ultimate Reality, the Truth, reveals itself in all its Splendour.

Such is the truth, the real meaning of the apocalypse.

The ego, death

*I*t is written on a wall of the great Wise Man Sri Ramana Maharshi's ashram, at the foot of the sacred mountain Arunachala in the south of India: 'the ego is the root of all evils'.

From our earliest days our ego, our human personality, must develop in order to survive in this world, in which we have to live from our birth to our death. The child grows up and develops its ego, asserting its personality and its difference more and more.

Then, when we are adults, our ego strengthens even more. We want to be the biggest, the most beautiful, the strongest, the bravest, the richest, the happiest, the star admired and recognised by all.

Our desire for recognition, wealth and satisfaction is insatiable. We always want more. We take care of our appearance, we want the most beautiful clothes, the most beautiful car, the most beautiful house and to have more and more money and power.

Throughout our life, we identify more and more with this body and this appearance that we have created to be seen by the world and to survive in this life. We create as perfect an image as possible of what we want to be and we identify more and more with this image.

Society incessantly tells us to be this or that.

But this appearance and image that we believe we are never satisfy us completely. There is always something lacking for us to be completely satisfied, happy, at peace and free. The more attached we are to this self-image, the more we identify with this body, the further we move away from our true nature and our true happiness.

And one day, what we call death knocks at our door and invites us to let go totally of our creation, this image, this little person we have cherished so much, this body that we have believed to be our me all our lives. The illusory me disappears into the dark depths of the unknown. We find it terrifying and unjust.

The Zen Buddhist monks of Japan have a beautiful expression to speak of this path that we all travel down at the sunset of our life: 'none can enter Nirvana who cannot pass through the eye of a needle'.

In other words, the ego, or what we believe to be our me, cannot enter Heaven. It has to disappear in what we call, in our ignorance, death.

So, what remains after death? Who dies?

The question we can ask ourselves all our life is: "Who am I?"

But the final answer to these questions cannot come from an intellectual understanding or a belief, a book or a speaker – it can only be found in one's personal Spiritual Experience, in personal experience of the Impersonal and experience of the Divine Self.

The ego and the body are not life, they are only a temporary vehicle for the spiritual being that we really are. They are a pile of matter which will disintegrate one day in the process that we call death.

Socrates apparently said to his executioners: he who you are going to kill is not Socrates but Socrates' body.

The spiritual practice or holy battle

The holy battle, the spiritual practice, whatever name we give it, does not consist in destroying other lives in order to enter an illusory heaven.

Neither is it a question of converting the other to our system of belief, whatever it may be.

The beautiful words of those who teach what they have read in books or what they believe they know can be beneficial for a while. They can bring a little comfort to a lost soul or pacify a tormented spirit. But they do not transcend the ego to reach Spiritual Awakening.

Throughout time and in all places, men and women have practised spiritual disciplines in the aim of transcending their ego and reaching the state of Perfect Bliss that we are all in, deep down.

Those beings that we call monks, pilgrims, searchers, hermits or ascetics have all followed and are following an intense spiritual practice to master their body, their emotions and their mental state. By daily and continuous effort and long meditation, they finally achieve total mastery of their human nature. They transcend their ego and enter the Pure Light of the egoless state, of the Divine Self. They are in perfect union with Ultimate Reality.

Those men and women deserve the greatest respect. Their disciplines and spiritual practices are the only battle worthy of the name, the only holy and healthy battle.

Like all of us, they are, or one day will be, Wise. Beings living permanently in the state of Pure Happiness, Perfect Peace, eternally free of all suffering, all desires, all attachment and all illusions. Whatever their physical and human conditions in this world.

In the eyes of the world they are madmen, but divine madmen, since they live beyond the five senses. The Life that they live has no senses, it is not limited by the senses, it quite simply IS. Infinite, Unlimited, Indestructible, Eternal, Intense.

This is incomprehensible as long as we live in the human state of consciousness and try to understand things through our five senses, with our logic.

The battle is over for the Wise. For the ignorant, the path is still long and dotted with obstacles. But the Light is always at the end of the path. Through ordeals, failures and suffering, but also instants of happiness and peace, moments when we feel free, moments of intense love, it constantly tells us, "Look, you are already what, in your ignorance, you are blindly seeking. You are already this Love, this Happiness, this Peace and this Perfect and Eternal Freedom."

But can we hear it?

Such is the deep meaning of the holy battle or spiritual practice.

Life

One day, a very long time ago, when I was aged about 5 or 6 and in the first year of infant school, our teacher gave us a lesson on rhythm. She played the piano and we learnt to dance to the rhythm of the music. One day, she picked up a triangle and a little metal stick, with which she tapped two sides of the triangle to make a rhythm. At the base of the triangle, where the two sides were furthest from each other, the rhythm was slow and the higher she went, with the sides nearer each other, the faster the rhythm became. Right at the top, where the two sides met, there was no more sound or vibration. There was no distance any more between point A and point B.

Still today, I do not know if that teacher understood the deep meaning of what she did with her triangle and metal stick. I did not understand for decades, either. But the image was imprinted in my mind for ever. Probably without suspecting it, the teacher had just given me the key to the universe.

Only several decades later, having lived through the Spiritual Experience, did I begin to understand the hidden truth in this image.

The scientist Albert Einstein discovered that the speed of light is 300,000 km per second. In other words, light takes one second to travel through 300,000 km of space between a point A and a point B (the base of the triangle).

The space-time in which we and this universe exist is made up of dense matter and slow vibrations that reduce the speed of light, which can only travel at 300,000 km per second.

Now, this space-time in which we exist is the most visible, material and dense part of the Cosmic Universe; the one that we can see with our physical eyes and understand with our intellect and scientific instruments.

The higher we rise spiritually, the faster and subtler our vibrations become and we are in harmony with ever subtler states of matter. The less dense matter is, the faster light can travel. (This brings us half-way up the triangle in my example).

If we continue our spiritual progression, up the triangle, we arrive at the top, where the two parts join. There, there is no more point A or point B. No space or time. Light is simultaneously at points A and B. Its source is in the Unmanifested, the Absolute, beyond space and time. It is omnipresent. It is the Spiritual Experience. We are omnipresent. We are the Life of all lives.

In this state of being and consciousness there are no vibrations, only Ultimate Reality IS, the Unfathomable Silence that is Eternal Eloquence. We are no longer separate from other creatures, we are in Unity, we have become Whole once again.

Life is what animates all that lives, including ourselves and this illusory body. But this body is not life. It is only a pile of dense matter. A vehicle for the Soul. A garment that we leave aside during the process that we call death.

What we, in our ignorance, call life and death are only the two sides of the same Reality, which is Eternal Life beyond life and death.

Believing that this body is life and wanting to prolong one's existence at any price is tantamount to prolonging suffering because of attachment to the body.

Seeing life from a purely physical, biological and scientific point of view limits our vision to human consciousness, using our five senses and logic to understand. It limits life to its coarse, destructible and mortal aspect. It means having a limited vision of Life.

The further we rise spiritually, the more we open our consciousness to the Reality which is beyond us, the less we are limited in our vision and our understanding of Life and of ourselves.

The more our consciousness opens, the more we dispense with the illusion of believing that we are this body, the more we are purified and the subtler our vibrations become. Becoming ever subtler, we enter into harmony with ever subtler dimensions of the universe, invisible to the naked eye, incomprehensible to our five senses and our logic.

Until the day when we are purified enough, subtle enough to receive the supreme blessing and live through the Spiritual Experience, the Experience of Ultimate Reality, our true Spiritual Identity. Or, in the language of religions, to return to Heaven.

The Life that we live then is of an intensity and fullness which are infinite, unlimited and inconceivable in the state of human consciousness. It is eternal and indestructible.

We are then once more in Unity, Eternity and the Absolute, beyond space and time.

The Spiritual Master or Guru

*T*he Spiritual Master or Guru is not someone who has read a book or listened to speeches, then teaches such bookish or oral knowledge to others.

A real Spiritual Master is One who shows the Light. He progressively leads the student away from the illusion of believing that he is this body, this human personality, and takes him in full consciousness into the True Being, the Divine Self.

He dissolves our creation, the ego, the human me, and reveals through experience the Divine Self, our true and enduring Identity.

He does not develop the disciple's ego, but teaches him to transcend it and reach the egoless state in the pure Light of Spiritual Awakening.

A Spiritual Master or Guru can appear in human form, man or woman, in any material form or without form, as is my case.

When we are in Unity, everything is God manifested in innumerable forms. Everything can teach us something.

Only one who has tasted the fruit of the Ultimate Reality can know its true flavour.

The author of this book is not a master and has no intention of passing for one. He is simply someone who has had the infinite luck, the extreme privilege, the supreme blessing of once living through the Spiritual Experience.

But my gratitude is eternal.

Epilogue

*E*xiled from ourselves.

Our condition in the state of human consciousness is that of an emigrant who has left his country of origin, Heaven. The story of the emigrant is this long wandering through a cycle of reincarnations and successive births and deaths.

All along the way, we are identified with many bodies and identities. We forget our state of Original Being, our true Spiritual Identity. We long for our Paradise Lost.

When we are once again in the Spiritual Experience, we are what we have been seeking for many human lives, through thousands of identities and thousands of different things. We are Love, Happiness, Peace and Perfect, Indestructible and Eternal Freedom.

There is nothing more to hope for than what we already are. There is no goal to reach, we are the goal again.

No more belief but Absolute Certainty, Unmovable Knowledge, from the Spiritual Experience lived through personally.

No more desires, nothing to desire which could bring us love, happiness, peace or freedom, because we are Perfect Love, Perfect Happiness, Perfect Peace and Perfect Freedom.

No more fears, no more suffering.

No more death, because we have transcended the illusion of believing that we are this mortal body. No more attachment to this relative, illusory, limited and mortal identity because we are our true Identity, the Unlimited and Immortal Divine Self.

It is the memory, the evidence of what we have always been, of what we still are here and now and what we are for eternity. It is our True, Eternal Identity, beyond all our temporary identities.

There is nothing to be created which has not been created forever throughout eternity.

It is a remarkable message of hope from the point of view of human consciousness. The hope that, one day, we will all find our Blessed Being. It is the ultimate aim of all of us. It is absolute certainty. Our Eternal Guide.

As Buddha tells us, one day all beings will reach Nirvana.